For Deborah
~ D.B.
For Maddy
~ E.F.

LITTLE TIGER PRESS
An imprint of Magi Publications
1 The Coda Centre, 189 Munster Road, London SW6 6AW
www.littletigerpress.com

First published in Great Britain 2000
by Little Tiger Press, London.
This edition published 2007

Text copyright © David Bedford 2000
Illustrations copyright © Elaine Field 2000

ISBN 978-1-84506-699-4
Printed in China
2 4 6 8 10 9 7 5 3 1

LITTLE TIGER PRESS

It's my turn!

by David Bedford

illustrated by Elaine Field

Oscar and Tilly found a playground.
"Shall we play on the slide?" asked Oscar.
"I'll go first," said Tilly.

"I'll go now," said Oscar.
"Not yet," said Tilly.
"It's not your turn."

"That looks like fun," said Oscar. "Is it my turn now?" "Not yet," said Tilly.

Tilly went round and round on the merry-go-round.
"Is it my turn yet?" asked Oscar.
"No," said Tilly. "I haven't finished."

Tilly went round
  and round
    and round
      and ROUND . . .

"I feel dizzy," said Tilly.

"I feel better now," said Tilly.
"Can I slide after you?"
"No," said Oscar. "It's not your turn."

"Can I go on the swing after you?"
asked Tilly.
"No," said Oscar. "It's still my turn."

"Get off, Tilly," shouted Oscar.
"It's my turn on the see-saw."
"The see-saw doesn't work," said Tilly.
But when Oscar jumped on the other end . . .

Tilly went up in the air!

Then Tilly
came down
and . . .

Oscar went up . . .

WHOO!

Oscar and Tilly
played together
all afternoon.